W9-BVR-622

Margaret Hillert's

The Funny Ride

A Beginning-to-Read Book

Illustrated by Elena Selivanova

DEAR CAREGIVER,

The books in this Beginning-to-Read collection may look somewhat familiar in that the original versions could have been a part of your own early reading experiences. These carefully written texts feature common sight words to provide your child multiple exposures to the words appearing most frequently in written text. These new versions have been updated and the engaging illustrations are highly appealing to a contemporary audience of young readers.

Begin by reading the story to your child, followed by letting him or her read familiar words and soon your child will be able to read the story independently. At each step of the way, be sure to praise your reader's efforts to build his or her confidence as an independent reader. Discuss the pictures and encourage your child to make connections between the story and his or her own life. At the end of the story, you will find reading activities and a word list that will help your child practice and strengthen beginning reading skills. These activities, along with the comprehension questions are aligned to current standards, so reading efforts at home will directly support the instructional goals in the classroom.

Above all, the most important part of the reading experience is to have fun and enjoy it!

Shannon Cannon

Shannon Cannon,
Literacy Consultant

Norwood House Press • www.norwoodhousepress.com
Beginning-to-Read™ is a registered trademark of Norwood House Press.
Illustration and cover design copyright ©2017 by Norwood House Press. All Rights Reserved.

Authorized adapted reprint from the U.S. English language edition, entitled The Funny Ride by Margaret Hillert. Copyright © 2017 Margaret Hillert. Reprinted with permission. All rights reserved. Pearson and The Funny Ride are trademarks, in the US and/or other countries, of Pearson Education, Inc. or its affiliates. This publication is protected by copyright, and prior permission to re-use in any way in any format is required by both Norwood House Press and Pearson Education. This book is authorized in the United States for use in schools and public libraries.

Designer: Lindaanne Donohoe
Editorial Production: Lisa Walsh

LIBRARY OF CONGRESS CATALOGING-IN-PUBLICATION DATA
  Names: Hillert, Margaret, author. I Selivanova, Elena, illustrator.
  Title: The funny ride / by Margaret Hillert ; illustrated by Elena Selivanova.
  Description: Chicago, IL : Norwood House Press, 2016. I Series:
    Beginning-to-read book I Summary: "When her kite lifts her above the
    ground, a child takes a 'funny ride' as she views what is on the ground and
    in the air. Includes reading activities and a word list"-- Provided by
    publisher. I Description based on print version record and CIP data
    provided by publisher; resource not viewed.
  Identifiers: LCCN 2016020720 (print) I LCCN 2016001849 (ebook) I ISBN
    9781603579872 (eBook) I ISBN 9781599538167 (library edition : alk. paper)
  Subjects: I CYAC: Kites--Fiction. I Flight--Fiction.
  Classification: LCC PZ7.H558 (print) I LCC PZ7.H558 Fu 2016 (ebook) I DDC
    [E]--dc23
  LC record available at https://lccn.loc.gov/2016020720

288N—072016
Manufactured in the United States of America in North Mankato, Minnesota.

Oh, look.
Here is something big.
I can play with it.
I can make it go up.

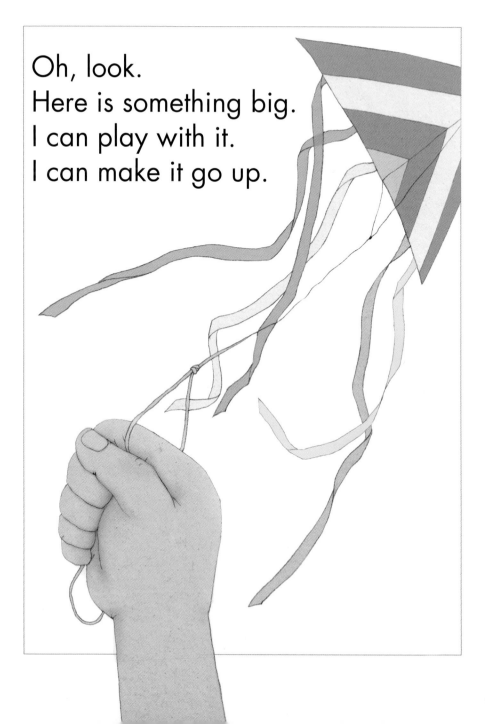

See me run.
And see it go up.
Up, up, up.
Look at it go!

Oh, my. Oh, my.
I can go up, too.
Here I go.
Up, up—and away!

Look down. Look down.
I see the car.
I see my house.
I see my mother.

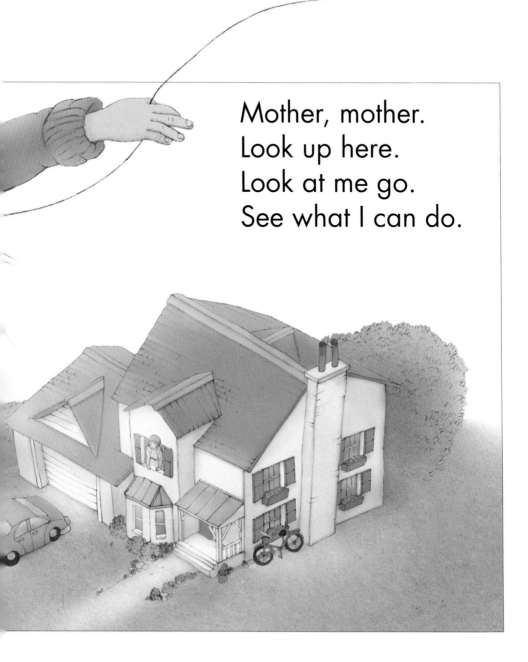

Mother, mother.
Look up here.
Look at me go.
See what I can do.

No, no.
You can not do that.
Come down here to me.
I want you.

This is fun.
It is fun up here.
Look at me go.
Away, away, away.

Now I see my school.
It is a big one,
but it looks little.

And the boys and girls
look little, too.
That is funny.

Oh, oh.
Something is up here
with me now.
Something big, big, big.
Do you like it up here?

What will you do now?
Where will you go?
I want to go, too.

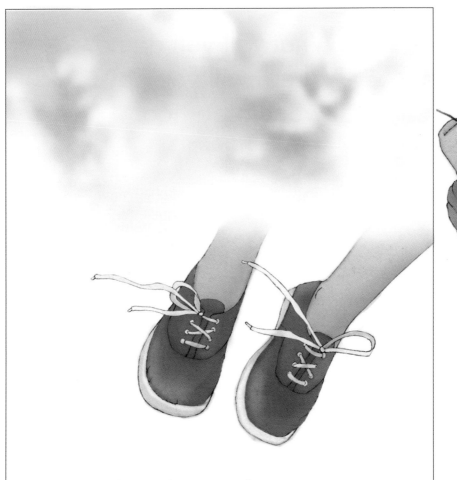

Oh, what is this?
I can not see in here.
I want to get out.

Now I am out.
But I am up, up, up.
Oh, my. Oh, my.

Look at that!
See it come down.
Down and down and down.

And now look.
I like to see this.
How pretty it is!

Here is something pretty, too.
One, two, three pretty ones.
Oh, my. Oh, my.

And look at this.
See what this man can do.
He is good at it.

No, no.
Go away. Go away.
I do not want you to do this.
Look out. Look out.
This is not good for me.

Oh, oh.
Down I go.
What can I do?
Help! Help!

Mother, Mother.
Here I come.
Down,
      down,
            down.

Oh, my.
What a ride!
What a funny, funny ride!

Foundational Skills

In addition to reading the numerous high-frequency words in the text, this book also supports the development of foundational skills.

Phonological Awareness: Syllabication

Say the following words, clapping the syllables as you say them.
Ask your child to tell you how many syllables are in each word:

funny–2	away–2	little–2	big–1	like–1	bicycle–3
popcorn–2	up–1	with–1	something–2	holiday–3	
pretty–2	school–1	mother–2	chocolate–3	pumpkin–2	
carpet–2	table–2	chair–1	fantastic–3	remember–3	

Phonics: Syllabication

1. Write the following word parts on separate index cards. Display the syllables for each word, out of order, and help your child put them together to make words:

fun/ny	a/way	bi/cy/cle	re/mem/ber
pump/kin	fan/tas/tic	pop/corn	hol/i/day
lit/tle	pret/ty	some/thing	yel/low
pup/py	kit/ten	care/ful	fa/ther
cook/ie	pen/cil		

Fluency: Choral Reading

1. Reread the story with your child at least two more times while your child tracks the print by running a finger under the words as they are read. Ask your child to read the words he or she knows with you.

2. Reread the story aloud together. Be careful to read at a rate that your child can keep up with.

3. Repeat choral reading and allow your child to be the lead reader and ask him or her to change from a whisper to a loud voice while you follow along and change your voice.

Language

The concepts, illustrations, and text help children develop language both explicitly and implicitly.

Vocabulary: Homophones

1. On a blank sheet of paper, make three rows by drawing two lines. Write the following story words in each row: to, too, two. Ask your child to read the words aloud. Discuss with your child that to indicates movement or action, too means also or as well, and two is the word for the number 2.

2. Read the following sentences from left to right and ask your child to point to the homophone (to, too, or two) that is being used:

   - I am going to the store.   Do you want to go too?
     We will buy two apples.
   - I like cookies, do you like them too?   I want to eat two cookies.
     We can go to the bakery to buy cookies.
   - My bicycle has two wheels.   My sister has a bicycle too.
     We will ride our bicycles to the park.
   - My class went on a trip to the museum.   The other class went too.
     There were so many kids, we had to take two buses.

3. Ask your child to make statements and ask questions using the different homophones as you point to the correct choice for each sentence.

Reading Literature and Informational Text

To support comprehension, ask your child the following questions. The answers either come directly from the text or require inferences and discussion.

Key Ideas and Detail

- Ask your child to retell the sequence of events in the story.
- What are some things the girl saw from above?

Craft and Structure

- Is this a book that tells a story or one that gives information? How do you know?
- How do you think the girl felt when she was going down?

Integration of Knowledge and Ideas

- What parts of this story could not really happen?
- What parts of this story could happen?

WORD LIST

The Funny Ride uses the 64 words listed below.

This list can be used to practice reading the words that appear in the text. You may wish to write the words on index cards and use them to help your child build automatic word recognition. RegulaSr practice with these words will enhance your child's fluency in reading connected text.

a	for	like	play	up
am	fun	little	pretty	
and	funny	look(s)		want
at			ride	what
away	get	make	run	where
	girls	man		will
big	go	me	school	with
boys	good	Mother	see	
but		my	something	you
	he			
can	help	no	that	
car	here	not	the	
come	house	now	this	
	how		three	
do		oh	to	
down	I	one(s)	too	
	in	out	two	
	is			
	it			

ABOUT THE AUTHOR Margaret Hillert has helped millions of children all over the world learn to read independently. She was a first grade teacher for 34 years and during that time started writing books that her students could both gain confidence in reading and enjoy. She wrote well over 100 books for children just learning to read. As a child, she enjoyed writing poetry and continued her poetic writings as an adult for both children and adults.

Photograph by Glenna Washburn

ABOUT THE ILLUSTRATOR Elena Selivanova graduated from the Moscow State University of Printing Arts. Of her many accomplishments, she is most proud of her contributions to a compilation of classic children's tales. In the last twenty years, she has illustrated over a hundred books and has created a wide variety of characters. Elena lives in Moscow and has an amazing view of what was once the estate of Count Rasumovsky.